High Note

orca
limelights

High Note

Jeff Ross

ORCA BOOK PUBLISHERS

Library and Archives Canada Cataloguing in Publication

Ross, Jeff, 1973–, author
High note / Jeff Ross.
(Orca limelights)

Issued in print and electronic formats.
ISBN 978-1-4598-1111-9 (paperback).—ISBN 978-1-4598-1112-6 (pdf).—
ISBN 978-1-4598-1113-3 (epub)

I. Title. II. Series: Orca limelights
PS8635.O6928H54 2016   jc813'.6   c2016-900473-2
c2016-900474-0

First published in the United States, 2016
Library of Congress Control Number: 2016931888

Summary: In this high-interest novel for teen readers, Hailey and
her best friend compete for a part in an opera.

*Orca Book Publishers is dedicated to preserving the environment and has
printed this book on Forest Stewardship Council® certified paper.*

Orca Book Publishers gratefully acknowledges the support for
its publishing programs provided by the following agencies:
the Government of Canada through the Canada Book Fund and the
Canada Council for the Arts, and the Province of British Columbia
through the BC Arts Council and the Book Publishing Tax Credit.

Cover design by Rachel Page
Cover photography by iStock.com

ORCA BOOK PUBLISHERS
www.orcabook.com

Printed and bound in Canada.

19 18 17 16 • 4 3 2 1

For Helmut Ragnitz, a connoisseur of the arts.
And for Megan, who has brought
so much music into my lfe.

One

Her voice was a thing of perfection. Like catching a snowflake on the back of your hand and seeing every little stem of it before it melted. I was frozen in my spot backstage at the Paterson Center for the Performing Arts. My best friend, Crissy, grabbed my hand and put her other hand over her mouth.

"Oh my god," she whispered. "Is that her?"

"It is," I said. "It's Isabel Rossetti." Isabel Rossetti is widely considered one of the greatest sopranos on earth. Some people disagree, of course, but at this moment I was ready to put her up there in the top ten of all time.

And all she was doing was running scales.

"Dammit!" she yelled. Then we heard something smash. "Never in my life..." Crissy and I backed up beside some chairs that were stacked against a wall.

The dressing-room door was slightly open. I could see Isabel inside, her hands deep in the thick curls on her head.

"It's lemon!" she yelled. The air around us shook with the sound of her voice.

Amanda Disenzo, the director of the current production, happened to be walking past. She stopped and leaned into the doorway.

"Is something wrong, Isabel?" she asked. Amanda is slightly short, slightly pale, slightly mousy-looking and, at the same time, absolutely astounding. She's what people call a firecracker. She became a director because she knows how to manage people. And in opera, a lot of people require a lot of managing.

"This is lemon," Isabel said. I could just see her inside the room. She was holding a bottle of water out before her, much like someone might hold a dead mouse that a cat has brought into their home. "If I wanted flavored water I'd drink a soda." Her voice was clipped. As though she believed each word was stealing some glorious moment from her career. "And I never drink soda."

I tittered, and Crissy kicked me. "Hailey, stop," she whispered. "Someone is going to see us here."

"I do apologize," Amanda said. "I'll get Catering right on it."

Isabel rose to her full height and held her breath before ever so delicately dropping the Perrier bottle to the floor.

Which was when I laughed. Because, judging by the look on Isabel's face, she had thought the bottle was glass and would make a great spectacle, smashing all over the floor. But it was one of the new plastic bottles, so it just bounced a little and then fizzed out on the carpet.

Amanda turned but, luckily, didn't spot us.

It took only seconds for people to arrive—two cleaners, another singer and Isabel's personal public-relations representative, who ran to comfort her.

Isabel was having none of it. She brushed the public-relations guy aside and grabbed at her hair with both hands again. "I need order to perform, Charles."

Charles nodded to this. "Of course," he said.

"Without order, everything falls apart. *I* might well fall apart. And you do not want me to fall apart. Because if *I* fall apart, all of *you* will as well." Her voice dropped to a whisper. "I do not ask for much."

"You really don't," Charles said. Then, turning to Amanda: "She really doesn't."

"And it is not as if I have kept my requests a secret." Isabel held up a single-spaced sheet of paper, full of text to the bottom.

"Isabel's dressing-room requirements are right here," Charles said, taking the sheet from Isabel and holding it out toward Amanda.

"I am aware," Amanda said. "As I said, I will have Catering bring the proper water over immediately." She turned and walked away, muttering under her breath.

"Let's go," I said when the coast was clear.

As we moved down the hallway, I heard Isabel exclaim to Charles, "She thinks it's just about water."

To which he replied, "I know. I know."

* * *

Crissy and I took the long way around back to the rehearsal hall.

"That was insane," I said.

"She's very serious about her water," Crissy replied.

The Paterson Center for the Performing Arts is a massive complex with studios, rehearsal halls, practice rooms, a five-star restaurant and a huge concert hall, where a production of *The Marriage of Figaro* is set to open. The whole building fills me with a kind of awe. I usually don't like to use the word *awesome*. First of all, it feels overused, and second, it is an ultimate word. Full of awe. Beyond what you would ever have imagined possible.

But the Paterson Center hall *is* awesome.

As we came back out into the main hallway, I spotted the rest of our choir. *The Marriage of Figaro* features a youth choir of peasant girls, and our choir was selected to perform in the opera. It was a huge honor. We'll be on the stage with professional singers, performing for an actual audience.

And that fact is also truly awesome.

Two

Crissy and I just managed to sneak to the back of the concert hall as Amanda and Isabel stepped onto the stage.

"Thank you all for being here," Amanda said.

Crissy grabbed my hand, and we sat down together.

"I am sorry to announce that one of our principal singers, Alexa Johnson, has been forced by illness to remove herself from the production. As many of you know, Alexa was to perform the role of Barbarina. I understand that many of you have been practicing Barbarina's parts. Therefore, we will be selecting Alexa's replacement from this choir."

There was no applause. A few gasps. I was a bit dumbstruck. No one had expected this kind of announcement. We were all in our late teens, and it was unheard of for someone so young to be cast in a major opera. Three of the girls turned to look at Crissy and me. I gave them a little wave, and they turned back around.

"This is crazy," Crissy whispered, nudging me with her shoulder.

"Seriously," I whispered back.

Amanda went on. "Though I know there are many wonderful singers here, we will only be able to select two of you for the role."

Heads turned again. I tried to keep my attention on the stage.

"We will need the principal singer and an understudy," Amanda said. "The understudy might never perform for an audience. Still, it's a very important position. Many understudies have gone on to have incredible careers. Isabel would now like to say a few words."

Isabel stepped forward and gave us a smile that lasted about half a second. "Barbarina was one of my very first roles and remains dear to my heart. This is a very bold move for the opera program. To have a complete unknown playing a major role in one of Mozart's finest operas is incredibly brave. In some ways, I envy whoever is selected as the principal." She stopped for a moment. "I also hope that the winner of this competition does not allow such an early success to go to her head. This business is more of a marathon than a sprint. Miss Disenzo has asked me to assist in this selection. Though there will be other judges, I know the industry. I know what it takes to succeed. I won't only be looking for a great singer. I will be looking for a singer, an actor, but, most of all, a presence. Someone who will take control of this role and make it her own. Someone who believes in herself and her abilities. Someone very much like I was when I first played Barbarina." She bowed again, holding her hands before her, and stepped back.

Amanda came forward again. "I wish all of you the greatest of luck. I have faith in this group and am certain we will find the perfect Barbarina."

There were more bows. More applause. And then shuffling as our choir director and voice instructor, Mrs. Sturgeon, motioned us out of the theater.

Sean Christiansen stepped up beside Crissy and me as we were crossing the threshold of the theater. "I guess the only question is which one of you will be principal," he said.

Neither of us tried to deny it. We laughed it off and kept moving, but I knew we were both wondering the same thing.

If you've never heard *The Marriage of Figaro* before, it's a pretty strange opera. Honestly, all operas are kind of strange in their own way. They're also seriously old-fashioned. *Figaro* (and you've likely heard this bit if nothing else—*Fiiiiiigaro, Fiiiigaro, Figaro, Figaro, Figaro, Fiiiiiiigaro*) is a comedy. Here's the story of *The Marriage of Figaro* in a nutshell. You've got this guy Figaro, who's like a personal assistant to a count. He wants to marry this girl Susanna, who is like a personal assistant to the countess. The problem is that the count, Figaro's boss, has been eyeing Susanna himself, even though he's married. Then this guy shows up who Figaro owes money to. By some bizarre deal, if Figaro can't pay up he has to marry this guy's old housekeeper! Add to this the fact that the count has a page, which is like a messenger. The page happens to be one of those guys who falls deeply in love with every woman he sees. He can't control himself.

The weirdness doesn't end there.

The page has been messing around with the count's gardener's daughter, Barbarina, and therefore is trying his best to stay hidden. And to make things even more strange, Figaro can't marry this guy's old housekeeper because...she's actually his mother!

These complications all come to a head in the garden, when Susanna and the countess decide to trap the count by switching outfits. It was apparently pretty easy to trap people back then. I mean, your wife wearing someone else's clothes is *still your wife.* Anyway, they catch him as he's putting the moves on Susanna. Then the countess forgives him for being a cheating jerk, and all is well again.

So yeah, not exactly a feminist show. But it was written ages ago. For that time, the fact that the women set out to catch the cheating husband was pretty amazing.

In our production, Isabel was playing the countess. Denise Cambridge, another fantastic singer, was Susanna. Denise was a star on the rise. Isabel, obviously, was famous, and her name would bring in the crowds. So it totally made sense to have a young singer in the role of Barbarina. This giant star, Isabel, was on one end of the production, and on the other would be an absolute beginner.

I always rode with Crissy, whether it was to a practice or a concert. My parents both work at a hospital. My mom is a surgeon. My dad is an anesthesiologist (the guy who gives you the gas to make you go to sleep). They are always late for everything I do. Crissy's mother, on the other hand, has dedicated herself to her daughter's singing career. She quit her job years ago so she can always be there for her.

On the ride home after the announcement, we sat quietly as Mrs. Derrick asked a million questions we either ignored or gave brief answers to. Finally, Crissy told her mother about the competition. I happened to be looking at Crissy as she spoke, and it was obvious that she was doing her best to *not* look at me. When she was done, her mother said, "Well, you'll absolutely be Barbarina."

To which Crissy replied, "Or Hailey might."

"Oh, I'm sorry, Hailey. I haven't heard you sing lately. Have you improved a lot?"

Mrs. Derrick is like that. It kind of bothered me at first, but I've become used to it.

She believes in her kid, which is pretty cool if you think about it the right way. If you think about it another way, though, she's not the nicest lady in the world.

"I've been doing fine," I said.

We were almost to my house by this time. I could see Mrs. Derrick wanted to say something else, but I guessed she decided to hold it in.

"You want to hang out for a bit?" I asked Crissy. "It's been forever."

"Do you mind, Mom?"

Mrs. Derrick looked at us in the backseat. She seemed to be deep in thought.

"She can stay for dinner," I said. "It's taco night."

"Taco night, Mom," Crissy said.

"Fine," Mrs. Derrick replied.

When we got inside, the house was filled with the smell of ground beef cooking.

"How was your day?" Mom asked.

I'm always being told I get my looks from my mom. She's tall and thin and elegant. My father, on the other hand, is slightly shorter, slightly thicker and the opposite of elegant. I sometimes wonder how they ever got together. I know, I know—looks aren't everything. But they are something.

I told my mom about the Barbarina role. Crissy added details along the way. Just the two of us, talking about our day. It felt totally normal. Like something we'd done a million times before.

Because we had.

We had a great night. We talked about boys. Watched a bunch of bad television. We even listened to some Katy Perry, which we *seriously* hadn't done in years. And when I fell asleep that night, I felt that everything was falling into place. That we both were going to find success one way or another.

Whoever got the role would be the winner, sure, but we were best friends, so whoever was the understudy would be happy as well. I was certain of it.

Absolutely positive.

Three

The ride to Paterson Center the following morning was mostly silent. Mrs. Derrick granted me her quick smile, the one she normally saves for cashiers and wait staff. She'd bought a recording of *The Marriage of Figaro* and was looping "L'ho perduta," Barbarina's only aria. (An aria is a solo piece for one singer. A lot of opera is about two characters singing to one another, but an aria is different altogether. It's the time that stars show their true abilities.) Each time the piece ended, there was a brief pause before it began again. In that moment Mrs. Derrick held her hand up and then dropped it like a conductor. As she drove, we listened to that aria five times in a row.

It was a brilliantly sunny day. The sky was a perfect blue. It was the kind of day that makes you want to run around outside for hours. Then we stopped in the parking lot, opened the doors and essentially melted. Sweat started to roll across my skin.

"I've cleared my schedule to come in with you girls today," Mrs. Derrick said enthusiastically.

"You don't have to do that, Mom," Crissy said.

It did seem a bit strange. Parents weren't banned from practices, but it was seldom that one actually stuck around.

"I want to see what you girls have been up to. This is all so very exciting." She flashed that smile again. It made me shiver.

"Whatever," Crissy said. Her mother bristled at that word but managed to keep her fake smile stapled on.

As we walked into the building, I thought back to my field-hockey days. I wondered if I'd been too quick to give up on that sport. Sure, I hadn't been the best at it, but at least it was played outside. Plus, you got to bump into people with force. The joy of clipping someone in the shins or stealing the ball away from them should not be underestimated. Generally speaking, physical contact of any description is frowned upon in opera. And opera takes place indoors. I'm a sunshine girl. Even on a hot day, I want to be outside moving around.

Sean Christiansen was waiting inside the front doors. I gave him my customary hip jam when he didn't move out of the way.

"Ladies," Sean said, looking at Crissy and her mom. "And Hailey."

I jammed him again. He deserved it. Mrs. Derrick ignored Sean—or didn't even notice him. This had been happening more and more lately. Some people were simply beneath Mrs. Derrick.

The inside of the grand hall was hot and gross. Mrs. Derrick spotted Mrs. Sturgeon and waved to her. "I'm going to go talk to your teacher," she said.

Crissy came to a stop a few feet away from us.

"What's up her butt?" Sean whispered. He flicked at his hair. He has a brownish-blond mop that he refuses to style at all. He spends an absurd amount of time flicking his bangs to one side. He also has really bright blue eyes. He's cute, something I am loathe to admit but he loves to hear.

"Mrs. Derrick?"

"No. Whatever is up her butt has been permanently lodged there," Sean said. "I meant Crissy. I don't warrant a hello any longer?"

"Did you ever?" I noticed Crissy had turned her back toward us. "She's going through this thing," I said.

Sean caught on immediately. "What kind of thing?"

"It's a girl thing, Sean. Why do you have to be so nosy?"

"Speaking of nosy..."

Crissy turned and glared at us. "I can hear you," she said. Sean and I busted up laughing. "What were you telling him?"

"Oh, we weren't talking about you," I said.

"No, not at all."

"Who were you talking about then?"

"I wouldn't want to say," Sean said. "I mean, it wouldn't be fair to—"

"Oh, shut up," Crissy said. Her glare finally broke, and she walked over and swatted the both of us.

"She thought we were talking about her," I said.

"I know," Sean replied. "Isn't it ridiculous?"

"Come on, we have choir practice in twenty minutes and I haven't had a coffee yet."

She dragged us backstage, where a large coffee machine endlessly produced disgusting, thick, beautiful coffee. I know, I know, all that caffeine and sugar is bad for you. Especially when you're seventeen. But Crissy and I first discovered coffee when we were twelve. For some reason, we'd forced one another to keep drinking it until we liked it. And now it's an addiction.

Sean, on the other hand...

"Disgusting," Sean said. "I mean, why?"

Crissy knocked back the first swig, then leaned against the table and smiled, eyes closed.

"Disgustingly perfect," Crissy said. I sipped at my coffee. There wasn't any milk, and with only sugar it tasted weird. I knew Crissy took milk as well and would actually be suffering through the cup. But her smile didn't waver.

"So," Sean said, pointing first at me and then at Crissy. "Who's going to get it?"

"Get what?" Crissy said.

"Um, the part? Barbarina?"

I could have kicked him. Sean likes to bring drama into the world whenever he can.

Not for himself. He has to keep his personal life as drama free as possible. It's one of the reasons he's never admitted to Crissy that he's in love with her. Though Crissy knows.

Not that I told her. I just didn't *not* tell her when she asked.

"April James is a shoo-in," Crissy said. She inhaled a laugh. Poor April had never wanted to be a singer. Nor should she have. But her parents, for some tone-deaf reason, thought she had everything it took and more to be a professional. We shouldn't have made fun of her, but it was too easy. She walked around wearing a Morbid Angel T-shirt. She painted her nails black and then had to sing the "Hallelujah Chorus" at Christmastime.

There was so much comedy in this world.

"Seriously," Sean said.

"Seriously?" I said. "We'll have to wait and see."

"Exactly," Crissy said. She pushed herself off the wall and tossed the half-full coffee cup into a trashcan.

Sean watched her every move as she walked away. It was pathetic. But then, most guys *are* kind of pathetic. Crissy spotted someone and took off ahead of us.

"Why'd you say that?" I asked. "Why'd you ask Crissy who she thought would get the part?"

"I wanted to see what she would say."

"What did you think she would say?" I asked.

Sean held his hands up before him in surrender. "You know she's going to be serious about getting that role."

"She's intense," I said. I realized I was defending Crissy. I often did this. That's what you do with your best friend. You defend them even when you know they're totally wrong.

"She's boring," Sean said. "You can't just focus on one thing all the time. Like, look at me."

"I'm looking," I said. "You sing and work at a laser-tag place. Am I missing anything?"

Sean looked fake sad. "How about all of me?"

"Really? What else do you have?"

He sniffed. "I like romantic comedies, pho and long walks on the beach."

"Sure you do," I said.

"You don't know me at all."

"Crissy is serious about singing," I said.

"She's going to be so pissed when you get the lead," he said.

"Who says I'm going to get the lead?"

We'd reached the grand hall. The choir members were standing in little groups of two and three. Except for Crissy, who was with her mother and, for some reason, Isabel Rossetti.

"See? She's too good for us already," Sean said.

I jumped in to defend her again. "She's a bit star struck is all. She's gone on and on about Isabel since we heard she was going to be in the opera." I considered stopping there, but something in my head made me go on. "She has a poster of Isabel on her wall."

"Seriously? Where did she get that?"

"An opera magazine," I said. "Don't tell her I told you."

"My lips are sealed," Sean said. "How big is it?"

"The poster?"

"Yeah, is it one page?"

"No, two," I said.

He left a long pause before saying, "The centerfold."

"Shut up," I said. He wiggled his eyebrows at me. "Weirdo." We watched as Mrs. Derrick laughed one of her giant fake laughs.

"You can almost hear the helicopter blades," Sean said. "Can't you?"

"Crissy wants the part," I admitted. "Of course she wants that part. Who wouldn't?"

"It's very dangerous, this wanting," Sean said. Then he lifted his water bottle and slowly opened it to drink. I hated how he did this. He always wanted to keep me waiting. As if whatever he had to say was so important that a few moments of silence would be absolutely fine.

Appreciated even.

"Why is that?" I said.

He held a finger up as he continued to gulp the water. Finally he set the bottle down and wiped his mouth. He was wearing a light-blue shirt, which now had droplets of water down the front. "Because wanting is the root of all suffering," he said.

I'd forgotten that he'd once again found himself interested in a philosophy. This time it was Buddhism.

"Okay," I said. "That sounds reasonable. I guess we should all just float along and hope for the best?"

"No, of course not. Do what you love, and the rewards will come to you." He bowed slightly.

I was certain this wouldn't be the end of the lecture. Sean seemed to believe he could drop pearls of wisdom and I'd graciously pick them up.

Someday he was going to make a super annoying high-school teacher.

Four

"Rehearsal time," Mrs. Sturgeon said. She'd come out of nowhere, and I jumped a little as she touched my shoulder. She kept moving across the hall, saying, "Rehearsal time," over and over again. Mrs. Sturgeon is a great teacher, but she has always held the false belief that our lives revolve around singing. Sure, it's a huge part of who we are, but for most of us, it's only one component of our lives.

Amanda Disenzo came in, stopping when she saw Isabel, Crissy and Mrs. Derrick standing together on the other side of the hall. She straightened her blouse, then walked toward them. I couldn't hear what was being said, but after Amanda spoke for a minute, Mrs. Derrick gave her a shocked look and nodded a couple of times. She slid her sunglasses back over her eyes and picked her bag up from the floor. Then Isabel reached out and held her arm. Isabel said something to Amanda. A moment later Amanda walked away, nodding her head and waving over her shoulder.

"That was weird," Sean said.

"I think Isabel convinced Amanda that Mrs. Derrick should stay."

"I think so too."

Mrs. Derrick and Isabel had another little laugh. Isabel quickly hugged Mrs. Derrick before crossing the stage and disappearing behind the curtain.

"This is going to end badly," Sean said. "I can feel it. Can you feel it?"

Crissy looked over at us. Her hands were behind her back like an innocent, precious little girl.

"I hope not," I said. "Is hoping okay, or does that bring suffering as well?"

"Everything brings suffering," Sean said, picking up his bottle of water. He took a sip, making me wait. Then he set the bottle down and wiped at his face. "Everything."

*   *   *

We shuffled into our places with Mrs. Sturgeon before us. Crissy normally stood next to me, but she had chosen to remain beside April on the other side of the group. I was about to cut over to her when Amanda clapped her hands. She looked down at us from the stage.

"Ladies and gentleman," she said.

Sean gave her a little bow.

"We are going to begin today with an audition for the role of Barbarina. We have some very talented singers here, but we need to narrow the field down to one primary and one secondary singer. I'll ask you to sing through 'L'ho perduta.'" She gestured behind her. "We have the score here, and Mark will accompany you on piano. Anyone interested in trying out for this part, please line up on my left."

"Get your skinny butt up there," Sean said, giving me a gentle push.

I wasn't entirely certain I wanted to. I wanted the role for sure. And it wasn't that I got nervous or suffered from stage fright, because I didn't. What stalled me was the way Crissy jumped up so quickly and shot over to be first in line. And then, when two other girls got onstage with her, she shifted position to be behind them. The other girls, Georgia and Karen, were not soloist material. Crissy knew this. She also knew that if you followed someone of lesser ability, it made you shine all the more.

"Go!" Sean said.

"You're making me want to stay. Everything you do forces me to suffer," I said.

Sean gave me a shove and kept pushing until I'd cleared the girls ahead of me and started up the steps to the stage.

The hall looked different seen from onstage. Wider and tighter at the same time. The upper balcony of seats was intimidating. Paterson Center was fairly new but had been made to look grand and old. There were golden spirals of carved wood along the walls.

I glanced down at the girls watching me. So many of them were here just for something to do. Or because their parents wanted them to be. I was here because I wanted to be.

I felt calm as I crossed the stage. I felt like I belonged here. Not as though I was some born star, but because I performed better on a stage than in a practice room. I loved the way my voice exploded through a hall, echoing off the walls and seats. I loved the feeling of pushing the notes to the back of the room and seeing the effect they had on the audience.

Then I saw Crissy and crashed back to earth.

She had that tight-lipped, scrunched-face look that meant she was calculating something. It took a moment before I realized what it was she was trying to figure out.

What to do with me.

She had been first in line so she could move to any position she wanted and give the impression of being helpful—kind, even. But we all knew going last would be the best. People always remember the final performance.

It wasn't as if she didn't know I was going to audition as well. Yet there was still surprise on her face when I stepped up next to her.

She shuffled to one side and said, "You go first."

Which really hurt.

She seemed to be affected by it as well. She didn't back down, but I saw a resolve in her eyes.

She was going to do whatever it took to get that part.

"It doesn't matter, Crissy," I said, trying to keep the hurt and, even more so, the anger out of my voice. "Go and do your best."

"We both know it's never good to go last." She held my arm for a moment. Her voice was filled with fake emotion. She was trying to sound kind, generous, good.

But I could see right through it.

I hadn't thought this process was going to be so difficult. I hadn't expected Crissy to turn it into a showdown.

"Oh, I don't mind going last. You were here first," I said. "By all means, you go ahead of me."

"Hailey, I insist."

I lightly touched her arm in one last attempt to stop this craziness. It was so obvious that it didn't matter who went first. It would never matter. But Crissy was making it matter.

"Crissy, you were here first. I'll suck it up," I said. She seemed confused. As if she'd had a plan of how this would all go and this wasn't even close to what she'd imagined.

So she switched to plan B.

"I have a tickle in my throat," she said. She coughed for effect. "Need water." She stepped out of line and jumped from the stage before I could say another word.

By this time, Georgia moved to the front of the stage. The piano didn't really make enough sound for it to feel like a real performance, but Georgia did her absolute best to perform. She didn't know all the words, even with the sheet music in front of her. It was in Italian though.

Georgia gave a laugh near the end and shook her head. "Okay, I'm done," she said, and she went back to her seat. Amanda applauded, and the rest of the choir joined in. Georgia had turned a bright red. If she was ever to become a performing musician, she would have to get over that stage fright. But most of these people would never perform. They would be teachers or choir directors. They didn't need to get on a stage and *perform*.

"Here goes nothing," Karen said as she stepped away from me. She had a better voice than Georgia, but she still messed up the words a few times. As she sang, I looked toward the wings.

Crissy was still there, pretending to drink water. Finally, as Karen sang the final phrase, Crissy slowly began moving toward the stage.

Karen stopped and gave an elaborate bow. The rest of the choir laughed.

"Well done," Amanda said.

"Not really," Karen replied. "But I'll take the compliment anyway."

Crissy was almost at the front of the room. Amanda glanced over at me, and Crissy suddenly stopped and leaned down to talk to someone. It didn't matter who went first. It really didn't. But for some reason I felt like forcing Crissy to go first—or calling her out, at least, for not going first.

"Are you ready, Hailey?" Amanda asked.

"I think Crissy was in front of me," I said, loudly enough for her to hear. Then I yelled, "Crissy, it's your turn."

Crissy did her best impression of a person taken by surprise. She held a fist to her mouth and coughed a couple of times.

"Sorry, Hay, can you go first?" She waved a hand in front of her mouth. "I have this tickle in my throat that won't go away."

"Absolutely!" I yelled. I inhaled deeply, trying to slow everything down inside me. To temper the rage I was feeling. To remember that Crissy was my best friend and nothing would ever change that.

Five

There were twenty-six people staring at me from the floor. Another dozen in chairs or standing around the outside of the room.

I glanced at the sheet music, then moved the stand aside. I was ready to show the judges that I knew this piece by heart. That I could do it in my sleep.

That *I* was Barbarina.

The music snuck out of the piano near the stage. It was hard to hear it, never mind sing to it. But I only needed to hear the first notes and then I'd be fine.

In fact, I was more than fine. From the first note, I could tell that I was going to sing well. I hit it dead on and sang through the first phrase with ease. I loved this aria so much. I'd practiced it daily for the sheer joy of sinking into Mozart's brilliance. It was short and perfectly constructed to show off a singer's voice. Dramatic as well. During many of the performances I'd seen live or online, a singer would be down on her knees or curled up on the floor to perform it. The audience would often rise out of their seats to see her.

I hit a couple of slightly flat notes, but otherwise it was one of the best renditions of that piece I'd ever managed. And I could see the people watching knew it. I glanced at Isabel as I finished. She nodded, more to herself than to me.

"That was lovely," Amanda said, a little surprise in her voice. I also sensed some relief. If she'd been worried they weren't going to find a Barbarina in the choir, that worry had been put to bed. I gave a bow as the applause rose up around me. I'll admit, it felt good. Not just the applause, but the sense that I'd done well. I'd nailed it.

Crissy was waiting quietly. She smiled at Isabel while tipping back and forth on her heels.

Amanda motioned Crissy forward. "Will you need the sheet music?" Amanda asked.

"No, thank you," Crissy replied.

I took a seat at the front of the hall beside Sean.

"Holy crapola, Hay," he said. "That was awesome."

"I know," I said.

"It's your humility I love," he said. "Such a humble soul."

"Of course," I said. "If you're looking for an interview, you need to speak with my publicist." It felt good to joke with Sean. I love singing and take it very seriously, but once I am done, I am totally my old goofy self again.

"Here we go," Amanda said.

The music began. Crissy listened for a moment. Then she dropped to the floor and knelt like an eager child.

She began to sing.

"What is she doing?" Sean asked.

"It's how the role is performed," I whispered. "Barbarina is on the floor."

Sean settled back into his seat. We could see Crissy well enough from the front row that we didn't need to be on the edge of our seats.

"That seems a bit much," he said.

I felt the same way but didn't say anything.

Crissy was doing well, though her high notes fluttered. She cleared her throat when she had the opportunity, as though that fake tickle in her throat was the only issue. Like a violinist with a slightly out-of-tune string.

She finished by crumpling to the floor as the weak strains from the piano came to a sad conclusion.

There was the same outpouring of applause I'd received. Crissy absorbed it for a moment, then stood. She brushed out her dress and left the stage to sit next to Isabel.

"That was very nice, Crissy," Amanda said.

"Thank you," Crissy replied, planting her hands on her lap.

Amanda began to talk about what the rest of the day would hold for us. As she spoke, Isabel and Crissy whispered to one another like school girls. It was only when Amanda finished explaining the schedule that Isabel rose and disappeared backstage.

Our choir rehearsal returned to normal after that. I took my regular spot beside Crissy. She bumped into me like she always did. Just a little nudge now and then. As though nothing had happened. As though she hadn't just used some very pathetic gamesmanship to try and show me up.

I kept seeing her dropping to her knees before she was about to perform. The vision ran through my head like a cut-rate movie. It was absurd.

We broke for lunch, and Crissy joined Sean and me at the food table.

"You and Isabel seem pretty close," I said.

"She's amazing," Crissy replied.

"What were you two talking about after you sang?"

"Nothing," she said. "Technique and things."

"Was she giving you hints?"

"Hints? No. She was helping me with the little things. You know, the bits and pieces I could improve upon."

"So she was giving you hints," I said. "That's cool."

"She's really nice," Crissy said.

"You do remember the lemon-water incident, right?" I said.

"She's at a level where she should be able to get the right water in her dressing room. Maybe the lemon does something to her voice."

"Oh, okay," I said. I was about to make a joke of it when I caught the tone Crissy had been using. It was the same tone I used whenever someone attacked Crissy for being, well, Crissy. She was defending Isabel. Defending her ridiculous actions.

I tried to let it drop.

Tried—but couldn't.

"I'd be careful," I said.

"Careful of what?"

We'd filled our plates and slid down to the floor to eat. Me in the middle, Sean on one side, Crissy on the other. Like it always was. "Just... I don't know," I said.

Crissy stared at the ceiling. Then she turned to me. "You understand who she is, right? You understand that we're getting to watch and learn from one of the greatest sopranos of our age. You understand what she could do to help a young singer. Right?"

Crissy didn't sound like herself. She sounded like her mother.

"You understand that she's a grown woman who throws hissy fits when she doesn't get her way, right?" I said, using the same biting tone.

"You understand that she stood on that stage and looked down at us. You understand that she has a reputation for looking out for only herself and no one else. Right?"

Crissy snapped a piece of celery with her teeth. "She is an incredible singer," she said. "That's what I understand."

I noticed Mrs. Derrick waving to her from the backstage door.

"I have to go," Crissy said. She gave her head a little shake and squared her shoulders. Then she glanced down at Sean and me. "Bye."

I clenched my fingers into fists and felt my jaw tightening.

"And there it is," Sean said.

"What?" I barked.

He shook his head and sighed. "The suffering has begun."

Six

The next morning I was waiting on my porch when I received a text from Crissy.

Can't pick you up this morning. Something came up. Sorry :(

I stared at it for a while. In the past I have sometimes replied to texts too quickly. Shooting something off that I regret later. So instead of replying with my gut feeling (*How could you do this to me? What is wrong with you?*), I took a deep breath and called my mother. She was already at the hospital.

"You'll have to take a cab," she said. "Use your emergency credit card."

"I don't know where it is," I said.

"Well, find it."

"I haven't used it in forever. Where's Dad?"

"In surgery. He's back-to-back today. He can't drive you."

"Aargh."

"What happened to Crissy?"

I didn't answer.

"Hailey?"

"She texted that something had come up."

There was a pause on my mother's end. "I think I saw your credit card on the hall table. The left-hand side."

"Thanks, Mom."

"Remember to only tip three dollars. It's not that far."

"Okay."

"And have a good day."

"I'll try."

I hung up and called a cab. Then I went back to my seat on the porch. The day was already warm, which meant the inside of Paterson Center was going to be unbearable. I found it difficult to sing when it was hot. I went back inside to fill a water bottle.

The Crissy I knew would not do this to me. I'd spent a lifetime looking out for her and backing her up.

I thought about the year we were really into Katy Perry. I'd loved her song "Firework." It was pure pop. Happy, empowering, a big blast of sound. Crissy, on the other hand, got into "Wide Awake." Of the three hundred million views of that YouTube video, I bet over one hundred thousand were Crissy's. She played that song endlessly, driving her parents insane. Her mother wanted Crissy to get serious about singing, and in Mrs. Derrick's opinion, Katy Perry was not singing. It was noise.

So Crissy wore headphones.

She listened to that song at night to help her fall asleep. She watched the video while doing her hair, making toast, even while sitting outside on clear, sunny days. It was all-consuming. My devotion to Katy Perry drifted after about a year. I still liked her music, but there were other artists I was interested in as well. Crissy told me she didn't feel complete unless she was listening to that song and watching the video.

She had changed her look. On the way to school, she'd duck behind the community center. She'd change her clothes, put on dark makeup and come out the other side looking like a miniature Katy Perry.

I'd stood up for her when people mocked her. I'd lied to her parents about what she was wearing. I'd told her she looked good.

Mrs. Derrick blamed me for Crissy's obsession. It was true that the first time Crissy heard Katy Perry was when I'd played a song for her. But I hadn't told her to go totally crazy over the singer and alter her entire life.

Still, I took the heat from Mrs. Derrick because I could. I didn't live in that house. I didn't have to be grounded or have my mother shake her head at me all the time.

A horn sounded in the street. I looked out to find a yellow cab idling at the curb. I locked the door, pocketed my cell phone and jumped in.

* * *

When I arrived at Paterson Center, Denise Cambridge was getting out of a cab directly in front of me. I'd seen pictures of her before, so I recognized her immediately. She was tall and heavyset. Her eyes were a deep chestnut brown that matched her hair. I'd heard her perform a few times already, even though she was fairly new in the opera world. She was the lead soprano on two of the CDs Mrs. Sturgeon had played for us recently. We had likely both run into the same traffic on the beltway and were beyond late. Denise didn't seem flustered in the slightest. I was stuffing my wallet back in my little purse when she stepped up beside me.

"Was that an accident?" I said. "I mean, did you see an accident on the beltway?"

"Yes, it was right in front of us." She was dressed down. Beige slacks and a blue blouse. Stud earrings and a thin silver necklace. She always looked elegant. I'd seen photos of her in costume and knew she could be stunning.

"Was anyone hurt?" I said. We began walking toward the center. There was no breeze to speak of. The air hung there, heavy with humidity.

"Not that I could see. I heard that someone mistook the gas for the brake." I liked her voice and the way she moved her hands while she spoke. She looked directly at me, but it wasn't creepy the way intense eye contact sometimes is.

We stopped in front of the doors.

"Hailey McEwan, right?" she said.

"Yes." I had no idea how she knew who I was.

"I was in the balcony yesterday when you sang. It was wonderful."

"Oh, thank you," I said. "I didn't see you there."

"I've been there every day," she said. "I enjoy waiting in the background. Wow, is it ever hot out here."

"It's going to be brutal inside," I said.

"I'm from California, and it gets warm there. But not like this. This is..." She looked at the sky. "Yes. Brutal."

"If it's any comfort, this is about as bad as it gets."

"What we do for our art!" she said, chuckling and raising a fist to the sky. The grounds were empty.

"I think we're pretty late," I said.

Denise nodded and said, "In the music world, those arriving this late can only be seen one of two ways." Her bracelets jingled as she moved her hands. The sound was soft and comforting. "First, as complete divas who believe the world revolves around them. Or, second, as disorganized, bumbling artists who simply don't have it together and never will."

"Those aren't great options."

She raised a finger. "But in the end, sometimes things happen and people are late. It's not the end of the world."

"My ride ditched me," I admitted.

"That happens!" Denise said, laughing. "I've had that happen. Also, cars break down. Elevators get stuck. Costumes are torn or stained. Life happens!"

"But then, those are all your fault too, right? If you were organized, then you'd be early and always have a backup."

"True. Some people, those who never run into difficulties in life, might see it that way. But you can teach them that things can be different."

"How?"

She leaned against the door as a breeze finally rushed across us. "You have to decide how you're going to walk in there. Will you go in with your head raised high? As if having people waiting for you is completely natural? Or will you enter with your head bowed, mumbling apologies?"

"I'm not sure," I said. "Which is better?"

"After how you sang yesterday?" Denise said, opening the door. "You're allowed one diva day. Keep your head raised and find your place."

I did as she suggested.

It felt strange. When we entered, the room quieted and everyone turned. I don't think I would have been able to walk with my head raised had Denise not been beside me. But as it happened, it seemed as though I'd come *with* her and not simply met her outside. The look on Crissy's face was priceless. She ditched me for no apparent reason, and I walked in with one of the principal singers. Isabel's career was on the wane, but Denise was a true up-and-comer. Isabel was seen as one of the grand dames of opera. A national treasure. But most of the newspaper articles about this opera featured photos of Denise. The old-school lovers of opera would be out in force to see Isabel Rossetti sing. But the future of opera in America rested on Denise's shoulders.

Mrs. Sturgeon waited for Denise and me to take our places and then brought her hands up in the air. "We're taking it from bar three, Hailey."

"Perfect," I said. I resisted the urge to apologize for my lateness and raised my chin a little higher.

And then we filled the air with Mozart.

I glanced over at Denise now and then. She was singing along. Isabel had disappeared almost immediately after Denise and I arrived, leaving Crissy looking stranded out on the edge of the group.

Sean nudged me during a break.

"Carpooling with the stars now?" he said.

"Crissy ditched me," I said. "I had to take a cab in."

"By *ditched*, you mean...?"

"I mean, she texted, like, five seconds before she was supposed to be at my house to say she wasn't coming."

"That's cold." I waited for him to go on about suffering. Instead he said, "Have you talked to her yet?"

"No," I said. "I'm not sure I'm going to."

He looked at me sadly.

I wondered if Sean had a secret motive for wanting Crissy and me to patch things up. He and I had always been closer friends than he and Crissy were. I imagined this was mostly because of the massive crush he had on her and the resulting awkwardness whenever she was around. It did him no good if Crissy and I were fighting. Not if he still had romantic leanings.

On the other hand, he was a good person. Maybe he just didn't want to see two close friends at odds.

"I think you should," he said. "You guys have been friends too long for something stupid to come between you."

He was absolutely right. Sean was very often, and very annoyingly, right. I decided right there and then to talk to Crissy.

We could get past this. I knew we could.

Seven

Crissy was always around Isabel, so it was hard to get her alone. In the end, I followed her into the washroom.

Crissy was at one of the sinks, washing her hands. As far as I could tell, we were the only people there.

"Listen," I said as she turned to face me. Then I stopped. I sounded like some authority figure who was completely fed up with a trouble-making student. Also, when you begin with *Listen*, it feels more like a practiced statement than a conversation starter.

And the truth was, I'd practiced nothing. In fact, I had no idea what I was going to say. I felt awkward and like the words wouldn't come easily. That was enough to make me uneasy.

"You know Denise?" Crissy said before I could figure out a follow up to *Listen.*

"We ran into each other outside," I said. "We were both stuck on the beltway."

"Oh," Crissy said. "Was she giving you hints?"

"What kind of hints?" I said before remembering my accusation the day before about her and Isabel.

"Oh, you know. Suggestions on how you could do things better."

"No," I said.

Crissy shut the water off and went to the paper-towel dispenser.

"Listen, Crissy, about this audition or competition or whatever it is." I'd started with *Listen* again. Like she didn't have an option. Like I was *telling her* how things were going to be.

"Yes?"

The tone killed me. I'd heard it before from her. It was the one she used with people she no longer had any use for.

"We can't let it get between us."

"Okay," she said, dropping the used paper towel into the garbage. "If you say so."

"It's one role," I said.

"It's a pretty big role."

"It's one role," I said again. "There are going to be more." Which sounded as if I was telling Crissy the part was mine and there would be others for her. I didn't mean for it to sound that way. I truly didn't.

"There are many roles," Crissy said. She took a couple of steps toward me. "I'm still glad I got you into this."

She smiled at me, and it felt real. Like the old Crissy was right there in front of me. She nodded to herself as though she'd decided on something. Then suddenly she pulled me into a hug.

It felt like everything was going to be okay for a moment there. It felt like old times. Then the door opened and someone came in. Crissy released me. "I have to go somewhere," she said. She held the door for a moment and then said, "Bye."

* * *

After Crissy left the washroom, I went to find Sean. He loaded up a plate at the food table while I told him what had happened.

"Maybe she had an appointment," Sean said.

"Lunch is forty-five minutes," I said.

"Okay, fine," Sean said, grabbing a celery stick from the veggie plate. "She is plotting against you. Her only intent in this world is to destroy you and all you love."

"I'm not saying that," I said.

"Then what are you saying?"

"I'm saying the way she said goodbye felt seriously final."

We took our plates of food to our corner and slid down the wall.

Sean munched on his sandwich for a moment and then put it down forcefully on his plate. "Okay. Here's the thing. She wants that part. We both know she does. She doesn't want to be second to you or anyone else. She sees singing as her future. This part could be a career starter, no doubt about it. That is all she's focused on right now. And your feelings are hurt because of it."

He flicked at his hair and smushed his nose. This is a weird habit he has—he puts his palm on the end of his nose and smushes it from side to side. I have no idea why.

"She decided not to pick me up today. Out of nowhere," I said. My voice was quivering.

"And in the washroom she pretty much accused me of trying to bring Denise to my side. Like there are sides."

"Explain again what you were doing yesterday," Sean said. "When you accused her of being coached by Isabel?"

"I was mad."

Sean laughed. "Everyone's mad at one another then. Hopefully, the final audition is soon. Then one of you can get the part and the other can feel wronged for a while. Maybe that's all this needs—some kind of finality. A winner."

"I understand she wants the part," I said, pretty much ignoring Sean. "But at what cost?"

Sean continued to smush his nose. Then he nodded his head as if an idea had surfaced. "At any cost, Hailey. She's a very determined person. You know that."

Sean was right. It was like a punch in the stomach how right he was. I'd been trying to convince myself that everything would change. That something would happen to push us together rather than tear us apart.

I didn't want to be in a competition with Crissy. But I knew that competition was at the heart of everything. Directors and conductors wanted the best. I understood that. And I hated it.

Sean snapped his fingers. "This story is about Crissy finding out what friendship is worth. That it's more important than whatever it is she thinks she's going to find once she becomes Barbarina in *The Marriage of Figaro*."

"What story?" I asked, glancing around to make certain we hadn't been teleported to a stage. Sean had a deep love of the theater and often wandered into detours about story and suffering.

"The story of Hailey and Crissy and the fight for the role of Barbarina."

"What are you talking about, Sean?"

"The moral of this story is going to be that Crissy comes to understand that friendship is more important than anything else. It's actually pretty Disney, if you think about it."

"We're not in a movie, Sean."

"I know, I know. But if we were, I'd bet any money that was the moral. Like *Toy Story*."

I decided it was time to try to drive Sean away from his weird musings. Luckily, he had a ham sandwich to deal with.

"Maybe I should offer to be the backup and forget about it," I said. Then I sighed dramatically without meaning to.

"Absolutely not, Hailey," Sean said, his mouth stuffed with lettuce and a dangle of ham.

"Why not? It would solve everything."

"Because this isn't only her story. It's yours as well."

*   *   *

When lunch was over, Sean and I were the last to arrive back in the concert hall. At first everything seemed very much the same. But then I noticed that there had been some changes. Crissy and Isabel were back. They'd rooted themselves in the first row of seats, about ten feet from the conductor. Denise was on the other side of the room, talking with a cellist. The choir seemed divided right down the middle. So much so, there was a visible line in the center of the room where no one was sitting.

"What is going on in here?" Sean whispered.

"I have no idea," I said.

"Parting of the Red Sea."

"Hailey!" Amanda called. "We need you up here, please. We're doing a run-through of the parts." I noticed that the full orchestra was here for the first time. Plus, along the sides of the hall and up in the balcony, there were people with cameras.

"Who are all these people?" I said.

"Get on up there, girl," Sean replied.

I walked along the right side of the room, because there seemed to be more smiling faces on that side. I tried not to look around too much, because the whole thing was really strange.

"We're going to get you and Crissy to sing alternating sections for Barbarina, if that's okay," Amanda said.

"Sure," I replied. I took my place at the front of the room opposite Crissy. It wasn't okay, I thought. It was a horrible idea.

"I've marked your sections," Amanda said. "It will give us a clear idea of what you are both capable of."

"Sounds perfect," I said. You get into a groove with singing. Starting and stopping is ridiculously difficult—but it is an essential part of opera.

I looked at my group of people. My camp, I suppose. I had most of the quieter girls.

Amanda was standing beside Denise. I saw that as a good sign—and then immediately felt bad for thinking that way. Crissy seemed to have roped in two of the costume designers and a choreographer.

And, of course, her mother.

The orchestra began, and Crissy turned to face the choir. She sang the first few lines perfectly and then for some reason had some serious pitch problems in the third phrase. She shook her head and stopped singing midphrase. The orchestra ground to a halt. She breathed for a moment. Everyone was watching her.

"Okay," she said. "Again."

The conductor, Evelyn Linley, started the orchestra again. This time Crissy shot through her section without stopping. It flowed perfectly, but I didn't think she meshed with the orchestra. It seemed as though she was using them as backup. Singing *over* the musicians rather than *with* them. It felt a little like listening to two separate tracks on a stereo, where each speaker is giving you something slightly different.

When it was my turn, I let myself sink into the music. I've always seen my voice—any voice—

as an instrument. The same as the violin or flute. It was my place as a singer to be a part of the music, not something on top of it.

When my short section came to an end, I let my voice drift into the orchestra's sound. Crissy stomped on her first note, almost screeching it. Sure, that is part of the opera. Barbarina is in turmoil in this scene. But it felt way over the top.

As Crissy sang, I started remembering, for some reason, all the sleepovers, the ice creams by the river, the secret crushes we'd had that we told no one but each other about.

The breadth and depth of our friendship.

I wondered what it would be like if we could swap nights. Take turns. Why couldn't we? We could flip a coin for opening night. Alternate every night after that.

But it didn't work that way. It couldn't. The cast needed consistency. I completely understood this. Still, I wished Crissy and I could share the role and the spotlight.

Cameras began to flash, and I realized the people lining the sides of the hall were from the media. Journalists, bloggers, opera geeks. Everything suddenly felt larger than it had a moment before.

Then it was my part again, and Crissy *accidentally* knocked over a music stand. I sang through that as though it never happened. Inside, I was steaming. I knew she'd done it on purpose. She apologized loudly, and Amanda shushed her.

The final phrase begins on a high F. It's a tricky spot. A singer can either float the entrance or hit it hard. The orchestra part is pretty sparse leading up to the final two measures and holds its chord right as Barbarina reenters. The voice is completely exposed. But Mozart also allowed room for the singer to add flair—to riff on a high note. When it came time to hit the high note, I nailed it and added a little vocal flourish on my way to the end of the aria.

I looked over at Crissy. She refused to look back, but it didn't matter. I had nailed that final phrase perfectly. I knew it would continue to ring in her head for the remainder of the day and deep into the night.

Eight

At the end of the day I went outside. I stood near the entrance and watched as everyone hopped into cars and drove away. A couple of people asked if I needed a ride, and I said no. Everyone knew that Crissy and I always rode together, and for some reason I didn't want people to think there was anything going on between us. I was angry at her and frustrated by the entire situation, but I would stand around and wait for everyone to leave, then take a bus, if that was what it came to. I wasn't going to lay our problems out before anyone.

It was nobody's business but ours.

"I have to run," Sean said as he came stumbling out the doors. He was fumbling, trying to get papers and binders into his backpack. Sean rode the bus to his part-time job at a laser-tag place downtown. He was always rushing to catch it, though it came at the exact time every day.

"Need some help?" I asked.

"No. I'm fine," he said. "Are you okay?"

"Yeah, sure. I'll take a bus or get a cab," I said.

He looked like he was going to hug me, but instead he bumped me on the arm. "You have to talk to her," he said.

"I've tried."

He held his phone up. "We have these awesome little things in our pockets. We can look at pictures of cats. We can argue with strangers. We can even call one another."

"I know," I said.

"I have to go." He finally stepped forward and gave me a hug. It was extremely brief and weird.

"Okay," he said. "That'll do." He backed away from me. "See you tomorrow."

"See you tomorrow," I said.

I was trying to decide what to do when Denise came out the front doors.

"We survived," she said. She stuck her tongue out like an overheated dog.

"That wasn't as hot as it sometimes is," I said.

Denise put her sunglasses on and stood beside me, looking out over the lawns. "Are you stuck for a ride again?"

"I guess I am," I said. "I was trying to decide whether to call a cab or take the bus."

Denise put her hand on my shoulder. "Don't ride the bus, Hailey. It's too much of a strain. Where do you live?"

"In Maclean."

"That's where I am staying too. Come on. We'll ride together." She hooked her arm through mine. We walked down the path together.

"Buses are a killer on the voice," she said. "The dryness, and all the people on there who may or may not be sick. I'm not being elitist, mind you."

"Oh, no, of course not," I said.

"Well, maybe a little. But you can't afford to get ill. You need to watch your health."

There was a cab waiting. We slipped into the backseat, and Denise gave the driver an address about three blocks from my house. Then she sat back and pulled a bottle of water from her purse. She took a long drink. Then she said, "So you and Crissy are good friends."

It wasn't a question.

"She's the reason I'm here," I said.

"How so?"

The air conditioning felt amazing. I leaned between the front seats to get a blast on my face. "She wanted to hang out more, so she got me to join the choir with her. I liked it right away and started taking lessons with Mrs. Sturgeon," I explained. "Crissy had been a member for a while. Back when we were kids, we'd always sing together. Mostly stupid pop songs, but I guess she thought I could sing."

"Well, you can," Denise said. She shook her head as she slid the water bottle back into her purse. "I don't like this competition idea at all, by the way. Not one little bit."

"But isn't that the way it goes in opera?"

"Not when you're seventeen years old, it shouldn't. You have to try out for roles. That's certainly a part of it. At times you know who the other applicants are. But there's never this direct competition. The back and forth. It's unfair to both of you."

"It is not a great time, I agree."

"And that act Crissy pulled today..." Denise stopped talking. "I probably shouldn't be saying anything."

"What act?" I asked.

Denise removed her sunglasses. "Her pitch problems."

I didn't say anything and must have looked confused.

"She did that on purpose."

"Why would she do that?" I said.

"To show resiliency. To show control. To prove she's the best person for the role. She made a mistake in an early practice, then came out even better than before. I've seen it done before. It's not only your voice that counts, Hailey. It's how you hold yourself. How you deal with the pressure. How you are able to recover from a mistake or anything outside your control. Isabel knows this. She's used that trick herself." Denise turned back to the window. "You need to try and stay away from this gamesmanship. It's beneath you. Beneath all of us."

She fell silent for a moment as we rumbled onto the beltway and hit a wall of late-afternoon traffic.

"If I could tell my younger self one thing, it would be that. Stay away from the ridiculous side of this business." She removed her sunglasses and took me in fully. "Yes, who you know counts. But who you *are* counts more." She patted my knee. "Remember that."

The taxi dropped me off at home first. I thanked Denise for the ride. She gave me her cell number in case I needed a lift in the morning. I stood there and stared at her number as the cab drove away. I couldn't believe everything that was happening. It was as if I'd been picked up and placed on a different level than I'd even known existed.

I went inside and sat on the couch for a moment. I had my phone in my hand. It would be simple enough to call Crissy and talk to her. We'd been friends so long that something like this shouldn't get between us. I knew it in my heart and in my mind. But for some reason I didn't want to hear her voice right then.

So I texted her. **Pick me up tomorrow?** I set my phone on our glass coffee table and looked out the window. It took a couple of minutes, but eventually she wrote back.

Going really early. Sorry.

I quickly wrote, **That's okay. I can go in early.**

There was a long delay.

Mom says no. Sorry, Hay. :(

And that was it.

I could have got angry.

I could have called her and yelled, or even texted hurtful things. But if she was going to be this way, I decided, then the competition was fully and truly on.

She'd made a choice.

I got out the sheet music for *The Marriage of Figaro* and found the CD I used to practice. Then I spent the next hour making sure I knew every note as if it were written on my tongue. I rolled the low notes, held tight to the midrange and destroyed the high notes.

Everyone loves the high notes. If you can hit those, you can turn people to mush.

Nine

I practiced "L'ho perduta" again in the morning, and while my mother hurriedly drove me to practice I listened to it on my phone.

When the door to Paterson Center closed behind me, all the noise of the world disappeared. It felt strange to be in the concert hall alone. I walked the length of the room and, without thinking about it, hopped up onto the stage.

Then I sang a few bars. The sound in that space was beautiful. The quietest note filled the room with energy and power. I did it again, closing my eyes and singing a couple more bars. When I opened my eyes, Isabel, Crissy and Mrs. Derrick were standing at the rear of the room.

"Hailey, dear," Mrs. Derrick called, "you're not supposed to be on the stage right now."

I stayed still, like a small woodland animal who believes that if she doesn't move, no one will see her.

"Really, Hailey. Rehearsal hasn't begun. There are rules, you know." Mrs. Derrick moved toward the stage as a group of kids came through the door behind her. "Come along now, hop on down."

"Okay," I said.

Mrs. Derrick had already made it to the stage. She reached up toward me. More kids were coming through the doors as she grabbed my arm and pulled me forward. I stumbled a bit, falling first into a sitting position on the stage and then, very quickly, down onto the floor.

Mrs. Derrick was above me, still holding my arm. She looked flustered.

"The rules here are that no students are to be on the stage prior to rehearsal." She pointed at the orchestra area. "There is too much that can be broken."

I shook my arm until she let go and then stood. "Thanks so much for reminding me," I said. I glanced past her to where Crissy stood, rooted like an old tree beside Isabel.

Mrs. Derrick turned and walked away. It would have been embarrassing had I simply fallen on my own—but Mrs. Derrick had actually yanked me from the stage. The kids who had seen what happened watched her walk back to Isabel and Crissy. No one said a word until the three of them had left, and then the room filled with the normal chatting and noise.

Sean rushed up to the stage. "Did I actually see what I think I saw?" he asked.

"Did you see Crissy's mom yanking me off the stage?"

"I did."

"Then you saw exactly what you thought you saw."

"Seriously, what the hell?"

Amanda came out from backstage as the orchestra was setting up.

"What's the orchestra doing here?" I asked. A few of the musicians looked tired. Almost all of them were carrying coffee cups. The double-bass player was nearly dragging his case across the room. They must have had a performance the night before. Normally, they arrived after lunch when they'd performed the night before.

Then a second wave of people came through the doors—the journalists. Two men came in carrying big, heavy-looking video cameras. The entire place had exploded in activity in the matter of fifteen minutes.

Amanda was suddenly beside me. "Oh, there you are, Hailey. We need to select our Barbarina principal today. Are you okay with singing all of 'L'ho perduta'?"

"Right now?"

She checked her watch. "In half an hour or so?"

I didn't leave any space for her to worry about me. I quickly said, "Absolutely. I can't wait." I thought of what Denise had said—who you know is important, but knowing who you are is even more important.

I couldn't wait to get back on that stage.

"Now, where is Crissy?" Amanda said as she walked away.

"You're going to kill it," Sean said.

"I am. It's going to be dead when I'm done."

"Destroyed under a mountain of awesome."

"Wiped out like a sand castle when the waves come in."

"What are we talking about?" Sean said.

"I have no idea."

* * *

It took almost an hour for the orchestra to settle in and run through "L'ho perduta" once. During this time Crissy and I remained on opposite sides of the room. It felt like we were about to engage in some kind of old-time rumble. *The Outsiders* came to mind, though I couldn't figure out if I was a preppy or a greaser.

When it was time to audition, Amanda asked Crissy to go first. Crissy looked to her mom and Isabel, then walked to the stage.

"Just sing—we don't need any acting at this stage," Amanda said.

"Okay. Thank you," Crissy replied. She mounted the stage, held her hands stiffly at her sides and waited for the music to roll up around her. Cameras flashed. The quiet conversations that had been moving through the room died down.

Then someone in the orchestra dropped something, and the music ground to a halt.

"Sorry," a violinist said, retrieving his bow. "Sorry, sorry, sorry. Not enough coffee yet."

Everyone laughed.

"Or maybe too much!" someone else called out, which created more laughter.

"Are we ready?" the first violinist asked before counting them in. I guessed the conductor wasn't forced to come in early for these things, so the first violinist had to pick up the slack.

The music began again, and Crissy went through the same process of flattening her skirt and then primly and stiffly holding her hands at her sides.

She did a good job. Great, even. She held the audience captivated for the full two minutes. She stood as straight as a mannequin as well. She hit every note with near perfection. It's not an easy piece to sing. It takes concentration.

I wasn't sure if it was because of how she looked up there, so stiff and proper, but for some reason her voice sounded different to me. Almost robotic. Not that there wasn't feeling in her singing. It was just very much on the surface.

When she was done, she gave a brief bow and left the stage.

"That was very nice," Amanda said. She motioned at me.

"Like King Kong taking down the Empire State Building," Sean said as I walked away. "Like Godzilla destroying Tokyo!"

"Same thing, Hailey," Amanda said. "Sing the piece—no need to act yet."

I thought about her words as I mounted the stage. *No need to act* yet. As if it was only a matter of time before I *would* need to act. Did that mean she thought I'd get the part?

When the orchestra began playing, it felt as though I'd slipped into a warm bath. The sound filled the space. I glanced around the room. A real live girl is before you, I thought. And she is about to perform.

When I began to sing, I did so quietly, almost as though I was afraid of disturbing the beauty of the moment. As my voice rose in volume, I felt the warmness I get when everything is flowing. When my voice and the instruments are weaving in and out of one another. "L'ho perduta" is short, one of the briefest pieces in the opera. But there is one crescendo that stands out. I had to do my best through the beginning of the piece to not think about that crescendo. As I'd been practicing "L'ho perduta" at home, I'd slipped on the first notes a couple of times. Even with the rising power of a crescendo, you have to work with the orchestra. You have to rise as it does, instruments and voice swept along by a slow, rolling wave.

The orchestra grew in sound and volume and dropped right before I did, so that my voice held the highest note a moment longer. It echoed in the space as the next line came up. I could feel the music in my chest, in my lungs, deep down in my stomach, and when the piece ended, I felt as though I'd been singing for hours.

There was applause.

Even a couple of cheers.

And then Denise was at my side. "That was beautiful, Hailey," she said.

I thought she shouldn't be there. Sure, other people had shown their allegiance toward Crissy or me, but it had been subtle. I would have been enraged had Isabel mounted the stage after Crissy sang.

But I didn't shrug Denise away as she put her arm around my shoulders and led me from the stage. "Absolutely stunning," she said.

* * *

It took more than an hour for the judges to decide who would be the principal. I don't know what took so long. I guess no decision is easy in this kind of situation.

Amanda took to the stage as the noise in the room rose, then fell to silence.

"We have had a very difficult decision to make," she said. Cameras flashed. "But we have finally managed to come to an agreement. Our principal for the role of Barbarina in the Paterson Center for the Performing Arts' production of *The Marriage of Figaro* is Hailey McEwan."

I didn't know what to do. Was I supposed to get on the stage and bow? Amanda spotted me beside Sean and beckoned me up. The cameras flashed some more as I joined her. I smiled and gave a small bow.

Then I spotted Crissy. She was staring right at me. Her face solid as stone. A tear running down her cheek.

I felt both incredible and awful. Emotions tumbled over one another. The applause carried on, and finally Crissy put her hands together.

She clapped three times, then dropped her arms to her sides.

"Crissy Derrick will be our understudy," Amanda said. She looked around the crowd until she spotted Crissy. "Come on up, Crissy."

Crissy mounted the stage and stood on the other side of Amanda. It felt like we'd finished a boxing match. The referee was raising the winner's hand while the loser had to stand there drowning in her humiliation.

I was sad for Crissy. But we'd entered this competition knowing only one of us could be the principal. That someone would have to lose.

"Thank you, girls. Rehearsals start this afternoon," Amanda said.

More camera flashes. Another smattering of applause. And then we were off the stage, heading to our own sides of the room, walking away from one another again. But I could only feel so much sorrow for Crissy, because the decision had been made.

They wanted me as their Barbarina.

Ten

We began blocking the next morning. That's where the director gets everyone to move to different spots on the stage so they know where to go during the actual production. Barbarina only has a couple of singing parts, but she's on the stage for other sections as well. The rest of the singers had been rehearsing for a few weeks, so they mostly knew what to do.

During the blocking, the understudy walks the stage with the lead. That meant that Crissy was by my side the whole day. She would nod whenever a direction was given and then wait for me to move to the spot before stepping there herself.

It was awkward.

The first time we were free, we went and sat in the hall. Isabel and Denise were working on a scene together. There had been some disagreement on where exactly they should be standing during this particular piece. Isabel believed she should be at the front of the stage, even though Denise was singing the majority of the part. The director was attempting to figure out a way to make them both happy, which seemed pretty much impossible.

"This is so cool," I whispered to Crissy. I had to try.

"I guess," she replied. That was all she'd said to me beyond a hi first thing in the morning.

"Isabel is really good."

"She's the best," Crissy said.

"Denise is incredible as well," I said.

"She's fine."

I was going to leave it at that, but somehow I couldn't. "There are going to be other parts that *you* will get," I said. "I mean, I know it."

Crissy slowly turned toward me.

"I should have had this part," she said in a low growl. "I've been singing for way longer than you have. I have the better voice. Isabel said so. But now I have to walk around behind you? Be your understudy?" She paused.

I had nothing to say in response. Her tone was angry and hurtful.

"I'm stuck having to say that the first role I ever went for I didn't get. People ask, you know. And with the press here and everything..." She crossed her arms and fell into her seat. "I mean, what do you even care?"

"What do you mean?"

"I mean, I want to be a singer. I am *going* to be a singer. This is my career. What is it to you? A hobby? Something fun to do? Why'd you even have to start?"

"Because you asked me to," I said, stunned.

"Well, I shouldn't have," she said. "I wish I hadn't." She glanced at me, then turned away and stared at the stage.

"Crissy," I said, "I—"

"Just forget it, Hailey. Just...I don't know, do what you always do."

"What do I always do?"

"You decide to do something, like soccer or field hockey or animation, and you're really good at it right away, because everything is easy for you, for some reason. Then, as soon as it gets hard, you quit." She glared at me again. "Can it get really hard for you soon? Please? Could you quit now and move on to whatever it is you're going to do next?"

I sat there, unable to speak. Barely able to breathe. Was this really what she felt?

"I want to be a singer," I said, because I couldn't think of any other response.

"Sure you do," Crissy said, standing. "Until you want to be something else."

I watched her walk to the rear of the hall and head outside. I considered going after her. To plead my case. To tell her she was wrong. That singing wasn't something I only did for fun. It wasn't like soccer or animation or whatever. It was going to be *my* career as well. But I couldn't put the words together. I couldn't figure out how to say anything to her without getting angry.

I rose up out of my seat twice but sat back down both times. Chasing after her to try to convince her she was wrong was the worst thing I could do. It would be an argument, nothing more.

There was no way I could win.

* * *

Crissy was silent the next time we were needed onstage. Then it was lunchtime, and she disappeared again. I didn't go looking for her.

Amanda had picked three parts to be looked at during the afternoon rehearsal. The first was a busy scene at the beginning of the opera, in which almost all of the singers are onstage at some point or other. The next was an aria that Isabel sang. And the final piece was "L'ho perduta."

Now that the full orchestra was involved, the understudies were left to sit in the hall with the choir.

Isabel was onstage, about to start her aria. The orchestra had already played through the piece twice, though it didn't seem to me that they needed to. They sounded amazing. Everything was tight and crisp. Evelyn Linley, the conductor, signaled the orchestra to play again, and Isabel began.

Isabel made it about three bars before Evelyn crossed the stage, waving her arms. "Not like that," she said. She stepped close to Isabel and spoke quietly. Isabel nodded. She seemed to be taking the direction well.

Evelyn started the orchestra again. This time Isabel moved differently, and her voice projected out over the hall. I could see that Evelyn liked what she heard. Although she mostly dealt with the orchestra, she often spoke directly with the singers as well. She was a tall thin woman who was in no way intimidating, yet everyone listened to what she had to say. She had worked with this orchestra for years and had earned a huge amount of respect from all the musicians.

She knew exactly what she wanted—which left me feeling nervous for the first time. I couldn't help thinking about what Crissy had said. That I was good at everything initially, then gave up when it got hard. Was that true? I'd never seen myself as that type of person. Sure, I was able to jump into just about anything and be okay at it right away. But I'd never thought of myself as someone who quit when things became more difficult.

I watched Isabel as she started and stopped five times.

"Okay, okay," Evelyn said. Then she turned to the side of the stage. "Hailey, we need you out here now."

JEFF ROSS

I was shaking and sweating. It was so weird. I'd never been nervous before.

I stepped out onto the stage.

"You will be singing this from the floor, you understand?"

"Yes," I said.

"So you will need to project."

I went down on my knees, then curled my legs under me. It was uncomfortable, but if I was going to sing loudly enough, it was the only way to keep my torso straight and tall.

Amanda was suddenly beside me. As the director of the opera, these staging prompts were all her ideas. She placed her hand on my back and straightened me slightly more. "You need to be down like this, but looking to the top of the balcony. Do you understand? Where your eyes go, your voice goes."

"I understand," I said. I'd never tried to sing this loudly before.

"You will project?" Evelyn said.

"Yes," I replied. Amanda moved to the side of the stage while Evelyn returned to her place before the orchestra.

The music played. I waited, listening, then started to sing.

"No, no, no, no, no," Evelyn said, waving her arms and bringing everything to a stop. She didn't cross the stage to where I sat. Instead she yelled to me, "We just agreed you need to project."

"Okay," I said.

"Like a mouse!" she said. "You sound like a little mouse." She wasn't exactly yelling at me, but it felt close to it. "You are squeaking at us. You need to *sing*. Loudly, with passion."

The orchestra began again. I waited, inhaled as much air as possible, and let loose with the most sound I had ever managed.

"No, no, no, no, no," Evelyn yelled. She flew across the stage and stood above me. "I didn't ask you to shout at us. I asked you to sing with passion."

"Sorry," I said.

"Don't be sorry, Hailey. Be better." She stepped away and motioned at the orchestra.

I was shaking as the music started again. Mrs. Sturgeon sometimes got frustrated with us, but she never yelled. She was always encouraging.

Then I glanced at the small audience and spotted Crissy there. She was leaning forward in her seat, her arms crossed and resting on the back of the seat in front of her. She was glowing, as if this was the greatest performance she'd ever seen. She was enjoying every second of my discomfort.

The first notes trickled out. I glanced at Amanda. She rotated her arms, pushing me to continue. And somehow the sound came. I directed the music toward the balcony. My lungs felt as if they were going to burst. I glanced over at Amanda, and the sound dropped. She pointed to the balcony and yelled, "To the rafters!"

I looked back at the balcony, and my voice soared toward it. I could almost see the notes floating up and out above me. I didn't look at Amanda for the rest of the piece. At the end, the orchestra kind of fell away, not coming to a tight stop.

"Fine," Evelyn said, stepping away from her spot before the orchestra. She glanced at her watch. "The singers can go. I need to work with the orchestra now."

When I looked down at the seats, Crissy was gone. I felt for a moment as if I'd beaten her.

As if I'd blown her out of the room with my voice.

Amanda stopped me as I was heading out the door. "Hailey, you're doing great."

"Thank you," I said. But it didn't feel like I was doing great. No one had ever demanded so much of me before. In my lessons and choir, I was learning. With this production, I was working. It wasn't whether I would eventually learn how to sing an aria. I was expected to already have the skills and simply be able to change whenever something new was asked of me.

"I understand that tomorrow you'll be fitted for your costume."

"That sounds like fun."

I thought she was going to leave, but instead she stayed there in front of me, so I remained in place too.

"So much talent," she said, almost to herself.

"Sorry?" I said.

"You have so much talent, Hailey. Remember that. An absolute natural talent."

And then she was gone, and I was left wondering how far natural talent would take me.

Eleven

"**F**orecast today," Sean said during lunch the next day, "hot and muggy. But don't worry, folks, there's a cold front creeping in."

I was being fitted for my costume and felt awkward with him standing beside me. "I can't even think about it, Sean," I said.

"Crissy's never going to forgive you for landing this part, is she?"

"It doesn't seem like it."

Sean yanked on my sleeve. "This is too short."

"That's why I'm being fitted," I said. The woman who was adjusting my costume came back and tightened the corset. I wondered how I was going to be able to settle onto the floor with it hitched so tightly.

"This is too short," Sean said to her. She reached around and yanked at the sleeve. Then she went back to making it impossible for me to breathe.

"It will blow over. She's just hurt right now," Sean said, taking a seat beside me.

"Isabel's no better," I said. "Have you seen how she grabs me? I have bruises on my arms."

"She sure can complain," Sean said. Isabel had thrown a couple of fits during the rehearsals. Once, she stormed off the stage for no apparent reason, shouting about "that girl" as she went. "But the question is, are you enjoying yourself?"

I didn't even have to think about that. "Yes," I replied. "A lot." It was an adventure. I didn't always know what I was supposed to do, but it wasn't just me who made mistakes. The other performers did too. And I was okay with not being perfect. That's what rehearsal was for.

"Then you're doing it right."

The woman helping me with my dress gave my shoulder a squeeze. "This looks great. How does it feel?"

"Tight," I said.

"Then it's fitting perfectly," she replied before walking away.

"That is seriously tight," Sean said.

"Is it too tight?"

Sean blushed. "I'm not sure what that would mean."

"Are all boys like you?"

"No," Sean said. "Not at all." He paused. "Most aren't even close to this polite, kind, generous and handsome."

"Thanks for the warning," I said.

We walked back to the concert hall.

"Do you think this story still has the same moral?" I asked.

"That Crissy will decide friendship is more important than dressing up and singing?" Sean said.

"Yeah."

"I'm not so certain that's the moral anymore. We may have overestimated her interest in friendship." He looked really, really sad. Sean is more loyal than anyone I have ever known. Crissy had never been very nice to him, but they were friends. I knew her sudden pulling away must hurt him too.

"She unfriended me on Facebook," I admitted.

Sean looked shocked. "Seriously?"

"I went to send her a message, and she was gone."

He shook his head in disbelief. "That's cold. I want to think it's all her mother's influence."

"She's broken free of her mother's influence before." I leaned against the wall. Then I remembered the costume and bounced off it. "We're seventeen, Sean. You can't stay under your parent's thumb forever."

"That depends on how controlling your mother is."

I thought that being seventeen was also part of the problem. We were right at the age where our parents' influence remained a factor, but everyone was pressing us to figure out our futures. At the very least, we were expected to do a little planning. It was like living in an elastic band that everyone wanted to yank on.

We watched as the musicians took their seats. Crissy mounted the stage and stood on the spot where I'd sung earlier. She looked out at the room. Isabel joined her on the stage. Isabel said something to Crissy, and Crissy nodded. A moment later, Isabel sang a few bars of "L'ho perduta." Crissy leaned into her and sang back.

The orchestra was tuning and there were people talking, but the two of them kept going as though it was opening night.

"This is bizarre," Sean said.

"You don't say."

"What are they doing?"

"Performing?" I said. Crissy looked happier than I had seen her in weeks. She sounded great as well.

I knew she was trying to show me up—I could tell by the look on her face. She was trying to prove that she was the better singer. That the chemistry between her and Isabel was something astounding. But I wanted to let them finish. I thought that maybe if Crissy could sing to an empty room, she would feel better.

"Why are you standing here?" Sean said. "You need to get up there."

"I want her to finish."

"Why?" he said.

"Because she needs it. And what can it hurt?"

It appeared, as the orchestra was finishing its preparations, that no one was paying Crissy and Isabel any attention at all. When they were done, Isabel took a step back and clapped.

She probably thought other people would join in. Crissy bowed. Someone in the orchestra clapped too, but it died out quickly, leaving Crissy bowing to a complete lack of applause.

Evelyn thanked Isabel and Crissy for the warm-up and ushered them both off the stage. Now I felt sorry for Crissy. The whole thing had been a little humiliating. But she'd seemed so smug about her little performance that my sympathy quickly evaporated.

"That was really desperate," Sean said. "I kind of feel weird about being here for it."

"I know."

"Remember when I had a crush on her?"

"I have to look back in time for that?" I said. "Don't you still have a crush on her?"

"Not any longer. I had a crush on three-months-ago Crissy Derrick. *This* Crissy Derrick is someone else altogether."

The rehearsal that afternoon was a mess. We were supposed to run through two of my scenes, leading to the next section of the opera. But everything seemed to go wrong at once.

First of all, the costume felt strange. It bit into me when I tried to sing. I actually squeaked a couple of times. Eventually, Amanda came over and sat beside me.

"What's going on, Hailey?"

"Sorry," I said. I didn't want to make excuses. That wasn't part of the job.

"Is it the dress? Are you feeling okay today?"

"Can we skip over my scene for now?" I asked.

"We need to see the flow from one section to the next, Hailey. We need to make sure everything is coherent."

I glanced out into the hall and spotted Crissy standing in front of the first row, her hands behind her back. She widened her eyes at me as I spotted her.

"I'm fine," I said. "Let's try again."

Amanda gave my shoulder a squeeze and stood. "Let's try it again," she called to Evelyn.

The orchestra resumed. I looked directly at Crissy as I began. Her posture remained the same until about the halfway point of the scene.

I was singing well. I hadn't made any squeaks or really faltered in any way. And as she watched me, Crissy's shoulders dropped. Her knees bent slightly. When I finished and the cast for the next scene came onto the stage, Crissy just stayed there. Not moving. Not even shifting.

I slipped between the curtains to the wings and found myself in the darkness. The orchestra moved on to the next piece. I looked out at the audience. Crissy was still standing there, her hands behind her back, her chin held high, and for some reason, she was smiling.

Twelve

We were given a break over the weekend. I slept in hard on Saturday morning and didn't bother to check my phone until the middle of the afternoon. When I finally turned it on, I was seriously surprised to find a text from Crissy. **Dinner at the Diner?**

It was so unexpected that I wondered if it was a joke. I let it sit for a moment. I thought back to how Crissy had looked at me the day before. She hadn't said more than a dozen words to me all week and now, out of nowhere, she wanted to go for dinner?

I texted back: **Seriously?**

It's been too long, she texted back.

I stared at this response for a good half minute. The Diner used to be our favorite restaurant...

My phone vibrated again. **Cleary wants to come as well.**

Cleary Hewson?

Cleary Hewson? I texted.

Yeah. She says she really misses us.

I hadn't spoken to Cleary in the better part of a year. There was no rift. No real reason. We just ran in different circles now and rarely saw one another. Back in grade school, Crissy, Cleary and I were always together. We'd even made shirts with *CCH* on the front. But that was ages ago.

I dropped my phone on my bed and picked up the stack of photos on my dresser. I flicked through them until I found the one I was looking for. It was from almost two years ago. It was the last day of school, and Crissy, Cleary and I had run into one another on the way out. I'd been part of the yearbook committee, so I'd had my camera with me. We still used film cameras then. The school had since removed the darkroom, meaning that the photo I had in my hand could have been one of the last ones ever developed there.

We looked happy. And not just last-day-of-school happy. We looked like we were the best of friends, lined up beside one another being completely goofy.

We looked like three little kids.

I finally texted Crissy back. **Did she contact you?**

Yeah, she called me.

And you want to go to the Diner? The three of us?

There was a long pause after I sent this.

Then the reply: **I really miss the way we used to be.**

I thought about that for a moment. I stared out the window at the well-trimmed lawns. The Subarus and Volvos parked in driveways. The teams of landscape artists working their way through people's gardens. This whole opera situation was only a couple of months out of our entire lives. It would come, then go. It was possible that Crissy and I would be best friends again. I knew Crissy. I knew she could fall so deeply into her pursuits that she could lose her identity, at least for a while. But she had always climbed back out again. She was entirely capable of being the person I'd always known. If this was her reaching out to me, I would be wrong to not reach back.

Ok, I texted back.

OK!?

ok.

This is going to be awesome. CCH rides again. Meet at 6:00?

ok.

I put my phone down and held on to the photo.

* * *

I walked to The Diner under a bright, early-evening sky. The day had been warm, but a late-afternoon thundershower had cooled the air. It was the first time in a while that I didn't feel sticky and gross. There was even a breeze moving down the street. And after all the time I'd been spending inside Paterson Center, it felt good to be outside.

As I turned the final corner, I noticed Mrs. Derrick pulling away from the curb. It felt like old times. Mrs. Derrick had always had to drop Crissy off after a rehearsal or lesson. Cleary and I had often had a half hour to ourselves, drinking water and watching out the window for Crissy to arrive so we could order. This time I was the late one.

Crissy and Cleary were in one of the large long booths against the back wall. Crissy was on one side, right on the edge of the bench. Cleary was on the other, leaning against the wall. They had water in front of them but nothing else.

"Hailey!" Crissy said as I approached. She stood and threw her arms around me. Her hold was fleeting, yet hard. Like she was grabbing on to me so I wouldn't turn and run away.

"Crissy," I said when she released me. I waited, wondering if she would say something about how she had been behaving. She flashed me a smile and then quickly returned to her seat. She didn't leave any room for me to slide in beside her. I sat down on the other bench. "Hey, Cleary. How are things?"

Cleary opened her eyes wide and smiled. "All right." She put her hand to her mouth and coughed. "Sorry. Yeah, it was good to hear from Crissy. I've been thinking of calling you two lately."

I looked over at Crissy. "Hear from Crissy?" I said. "I thought..." A waitress was at our table, pen and pad in hand.

"Can I please have a ginger ale?" Crissy said.

"Sure. What about you two?"

"Tea," Cleary said.

"I'm going to stick with water for now," I said.

"Are we eating here?" the waitress asked.

"Three grilled cheese and a plate of fries to share," Crissy said. It was what we'd always had when we were eleven or twelve. I wasn't certain I wanted a grilled cheese, but remembering those days felt good. I hadn't been feeling like myself since the opera began. I had never really been under pressure in my life before. Not like this. I was handling it, but I really needed some friends. Sean had been there for me as much as possible, but he was often busy. He was looking at expensive colleges and working extra shifts at the laser-tag place.

Cleary sneezed as the waitress walked away. She grabbed a napkin from the dispenser and apologized again. "I hear you're in some theater thing," she said.

"An opera, actually," I said.

"Wow, that's awesome," Cleary said, wiping her nose. "So you do lots of singing?"

"Yes, it's a Mozart opera. *The Marriage of Figaro.*"

"That's the one that Bugs Bunny does, right?"

"No," Crissy said, jumping into the conversation. "That's *The Barber of Seville.*"

Cleary sneezed again. Her eyes and nose were red.

"I don't remember you having allergies," I said.

"It's all about this count," Crissy said before Cleary could answer. "And he has eyes for someone other than his wife."

"I don't know that one," Cleary said.

I waited for her to take a drink of her water and then repeated, "I don't remember you having allergies."

Cleary turned to me, blowing her nose into a napkin. "Oh, I don't. I was in New Zealand with my dad. It's winter down there. I caught a stupid cold. It's almost done though, I think." She cleared her throat, and when the waitress brought her a tea, she drank deeply and slowly. Enjoying the feeling of warmth moving down her sore throat, I guessed.

"New Zealand," I said. "What was that like?" I looked at Crissy again, who was working on her ginger ale.

"It's awesome down there. Totally," Cleary said before falling into another coughing fit. "With all the mountains and the water and everything. We went heli-skiing. I picked up something from one of the other skiers. It sucks, but it was totally worth it. It's weird to have a terrible cold when it's so hot and humid out."

"I bet," I said. I took a drink from my water and then excused myself to go to the washroom. It was around a corner beside the kitchen. I went as far as turning the corner, then stopped and looked back. From where I stood, I could see our table, but it would be difficult for Crissy to spot me. I waited a moment, hoping I was wrong. Hoping that what I thought was happening wasn't. But then Cleary looked out the window, and I watched as Crissy swapped my water glass with Cleary's.

I fell against the wall. I felt like crying. You can't write your friends off, I thought. You can't do that. I knew I should go back and talk to Crissy about what had happened. Maybe if we got it all out in the open, we could move past it. I wanted to tell her it wasn't worth it. That Barbarina wasn't even that big a role. That missing out on one part wasn't the end of her career.

But I didn't have any charity available. She'd stepped over a line, and I wasn't certain she would ever be able to step back.

It felt as though our friendship was truly over.

So I didn't go back to the table. I slipped out the door and walked back to my house, earbuds plugged into my ears, *The Marriage of Figaro* playing loudly, making the world and all the people in it feel like bit actors in the production of my life.

Thirteen

A nd then it was opening night. There was a kind of electricity in the air. Everything we'd been working toward was going to come together at last.

The dress rehearsal had gone off almost without a hitch. Amanda had sat us down that afternoon and spoken very briefly about what we could improve. We were all there, understudies included, when she came to me. "Hailey, you've proven to us all that we absolutely made the right choice for Barbarina," she said. "If you perform as you did last night, you will find glowing reviews in the morning."

"Thank you," was all I could manage. Denise had squeezed my arm a little. Then I'd spotted Crissy across the room, watching. She had her arms crossed, and I could tell she wanted to leave. But she couldn't. She had to stand there and listen.

Until that moment, Crissy wouldn't have known how well the dress rehearsal had gone because she'd skipped the entire week. Apparently, she'd come down with a cold. I didn't know whether to believe this or not. On the one hand, it would have been poetic justice if Crissy had actually caught Cleary's cold. But I had a feeling it was just another lie.

I really hoped that Crissy had missed the rehearsals because she felt bad about what she'd attempted to do.

* * *

Everyone was wishing us good luck as the members of the orchestra took their spots. I peeked around the curtain and found the entire hall full, right up to the top of the second balcony.

Sean gave me a bump on the arm.

"Nervous?"

"That's the wrong thing to ask someone," I said.

"Well, are you?"

I let the curtain fall back. "I wasn't until you came up here and started asking me if I was."

"Don't be nervous," he said.

Which was incredibly useful.

"That's easy for you to say."

"Nerves are the very root of suffering. They arrive as one is worrying about the future or concerned about the past. They happen when you're not thinking of the moment at all. If you get nervous, you will just *get through* this performance. You won't really be a *part* of it." He grabbed me by my giant poofy shoulders. "Be in the moment."

"You are tiring," I said. "I mean, honestly and truly exhausting."

It looked like he was going to kiss me.

"What are you doing?" I said.

"Looking deeply into your eyes."

"Why?"

"I want to see if you're in the moment."

Luckily, Mrs. Sturgeon called for the chorus, and Sean had to take off before things got any weirder.

It was strange to hear the chorus warming up without me. Normally, I'd have been right there in the middle of it. Instead, I stood watching, as though it was some group I'd had something to do with long ago.

As though I'd moved on.

They sounded great once they were out on the stage. Crissy looked miserable though. Her face, when she wasn't singing, fell in the same way as that grumpy-cat meme on the Internet.

It broke my heart to see her like that, but it was sort of funny too. She looked like an entitled little kid who hadn't gotten what she wanted. She was pouting, angry, and trying to make everyone around her feel the same way.

Before I knew it was happening, the lights went down and the orchestra began to play the overture.

People moved behind me in the dimness. There was an energy in the backstage area I'd never felt before. As though everyone was on the verge of exploding. The orchestra sounded amazing. And then it was time for the first singing part, and the performers slipped onstage.

I watched from behind the curtain until it was my time to go on. Of course, I stepped slightly off to one side and was blinded by a spotlight. I stumbled a little, corrected myself and refocused.

It's incredible being on a stage, singing with an orchestra. I don't know how to explain it. I mean, there's the music playing, the other actors moving through their parts, the audience there in the darkness before you. And your voice rising up above it all.

Maybe if Sean hadn't said anything, I wouldn't have been nervous, but I was feeling it now. My hands were clammy. My voice jittered slightly. Still, I managed to contain the nerves. I let them flow through me and out. I didn't hold them in my hands or stomach. I didn't let them get near my vocal cords. I focused on the music and what I had to do.

When it was over and we'd taken our bows, Denise dragged me to the front of the stage to take one extra bow. I held her hand as we bent, then straightened again. Denise stepped away, and the audience continued to clap. I bowed again, alone at the front of the stage, the spot-lights completely blinding me.

Everyone was standing. The entire audience was on its feet.

"That was perfect, Hailey," Denise said as we left the stage. "You did so well."

"Thank you," I said.

"Tomorrow you get to do it again."

"I can't wait," I said. I wanted to be back on the stage already. There were a couple of phrases I felt I could have put more emotion into. One section where I wanted to play with my volume to see if it would have a different effect on the audience. But I'd felt comfortable in my role, and though it was fairly brief, I'd tried to make the most of it.

There were reporters backstage. I was asked a hundred questions. What it felt like. How it was up there. Nerves, ambitions, the entire process. "What will come next?" asked a young reporter with crisply cut hair and deep brown eyes.

"I don't know," I said. "I guess the rest of the week."

"Perfect," he said. "A girl who focuses on the goal at hand. Let them come to you."

"I guess."

He winked at me. "They will—don't worry about that."

Later, when the reporters were gone and I was in my dressing room removing my costume, wig and makeup, Denise popped in.

She grabbed my shoulders and leaned her chin on my head. "Truly brilliant," she said. "I knew you were the right choice."

"Thank you," I said.

"It was close," she said, letting go of me.

I didn't reply. I was looking at her reflection in the mirror before me. "Crissy almost got the part?" I asked.

"The votes seemed to be going her way. Then it was tied with only one vote left. The final one was Clive's."

"The baritone?" I said.

"Yes."

I thought back to the auditions and couldn't remember seeing Clive there. In fact, I remembered Amanda looking for him just before the rehearsal that afternoon.

"I don't remember him being there when I auditioned," I said.

Denise winked at me. "That's because he wasn't." She leaned in close. "Isabel can't always get her way. When I discovered that Clive had been asked to be one of the judges, I told him the way the vote should go. He listens to me. We've been best of friends for a while now. He trusts my instincts."

"So he only voted for me because you asked him to?"

"Don't sound so surprised, Hailey. It's just the way things work. You *were* the better choice. Crissy is good, but she would have made it all about her. She would have turned into a mini Isabel. A micro diva. It's better for her to be brought down from the beginning, before she causes herself harm. I could tell you would be able to handle it. And you have. You're wonderful." She gave me a quick pat on the head. "See you in the hall for the reception, okay?"

"Okay," I said.

I sat there stunned for some time. I had assumed I'd won the part fairly. In fact, I'd assumed that only Isabel had voted for Crissy. I was totally wrong. It had been so close. I'd only received the final vote because of backstage politics.

I didn't know what to do with this information. It felt awful to know. It felt...wrong. I tried to convince myself it didn't matter. I had the part, and I was doing an incredible job. But it did matter.

It mattered a lot.

Fourteen

"Has Crissy forgiven you?" Denise asked when we were off in a corner at the post-performance reception. My parents were going to take Sean and me for a late dinner. I wanted to soak in the opening-night glory, but I could barely make an appearance before leaving. The real party, I knew, would be on closing night.

"I don't think there's anything she needs to forgive me for," I said.

"I guess I mean, has she accepted her role?"

"No, she certainly hasn't."

"That's too bad for her," she said.

"It is."

"For both of you."

"I guess," I said.

"You're hurt," Denise said. I could see Sean watching me from the doorway. "It won't always be like this."

"It won't?" I said hopefully.

"You're going to lose friends. But you're also going to find out who your true friends are." She put an arm around my shoulders. I don't know what happened—maybe it was the hugeness of the night—but I began to cry.

"Oh, sweetie."

"I'm okay," I said. Though, of course, I wasn't. I felt awful. And then I got angry, because on the night when I should have felt better than ever before, I was sitting there crying over someone else's bitterness. Crying over the fact that, yes, I had won the part, but in a way I'd never wanted to. Why did Denise have to tell me what had happened? Why did Crissy have to be the loser? Why did everything get so complicated and crappy right when it felt like my life was starting?

"It sucks," Denise said. "It really, really sucks. But it's not your fault. You know that, right?"

"Yeah."

"You had a great night out there. You're a star," she said. "You have an exciting future ahead of you. I can feel it. Don't let anything or anyone change who you are, Hailey McEwan." She spun me around and looked me in the eye. "You have a real talent. It's going to make people jealous. But that isn't your problem. It's theirs."

It felt even more horrible to hear this. Of course, it was true. I hated how the world seemed to revolve around competition. But audiences don't want to see second place. They want the stars. The most talented.

The best.

*   *   *

At the restaurant, my parents heaped praise on me. And it felt great. All of it. It was one of the best days of my life. But I still kept seeing Crissy's hurt face. Not because of something I'd done, but because of who I was and what I could be.

"Suffering," Sean said at one point, when my parents were questioning the waiter about the wine and their attention was elsewhere.

"This again?" I said.

"I've been thinking about it, and maybe the moral of this story is about suffering."

"Well, you've been talking about it enough. I'm sure it had to lead somewhere."

"You're suffering because you want things to be like they used to be. But you also know you have to look ahead. You are suffering because of the past and the future."

"That is generally what people do," I said. "We remember and we wonder."

"Ah, good. Yes, exactly. Crissy is suffering in a different way. She's suffering from wanting."

"Okay. But she brought that on herself," I said.

I hadn't told Sean what Denise had told me about the vote. I didn't think I would ever tell anyone. It was going to be one of those secrets that lingered inside me forever. The weirdest thing was that right after Denise had told me how the vote had gone, while I'd sat there alone in the dressing room, staring at my reflection in the mirror, the only person I'd wanted to talk to was Crissy. I'd wanted to tell her how unfair it was. How stupid. But I couldn't. I never could. Even if it might make things better, I was going to have to keep this inside me forever and never tell a soul.

"She brought it on herself," Sean agreed. "But it's interesting, because you are suffering in the quiet moments. The times when you're alone and thinking about what has happened. Wondering if anything might change. You're suffering because of the past and the future. Whereas Crissy is suffering in the present. That's a difficult thing to do. She's sitting on the side of that stage, watching you perform, and she's suffering because she wishes she was you. I doubt she's even thinking about how she could have done better in the audition or what might come next. She's suffering because she isn't you."

"You think so?"

"I know it."

"So do you think once this production is over, she'll come back around?"

Sean shrugged.

"I have no idea," he said.

I looked at the fancy people around us. The waiters pouring fine wine into crystal glasses. The men and women in expensive outfits. The chatter and laughter and delicious smells. This was going to be my future. I had no doubt whatsoever. I was here because of my talent.

I was here because I belonged.

"Sorry, what?" I said.

"You never know what's going to happen," Sean said. "That's the moral of this story."

"That's the moral of every story, Sean."

He shrugged again, then speared a shrimp with his fork and put it in his mouth. "Or it could be that we bring all the good and bad in our lives upon ourselves."

"That sounds closer to the truth," I said.

Because then nothing that had happened to Crissy could be my fault. And in the warm glow of that amazing night, that was the exact kind of moral that would bring no suffering to me whatsoever.

JEFF ROSS is an award-winning author of seven novels for young adults. He currently teaches scriptwriting and English at Algonquin College in Ottawa, Ontario, where he lives with his wife and two sons. For more information, visit www.jeffrossbooks.com

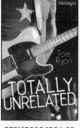